The Astonishing Case of the STOLEN STORIES

THE ASTONISHING CASE OF THE STOLEN STORIES
A JONATHAN CAPE BOOK 978 1 780 08034 5

Published in Great Britain by Jonathan Cape,
an imprint of Random House Children's Publishers UK
A Random House Group Company

This edition published 2014
10 9 8 7 6 5 4 3 2 1

RANDOM HOUSE CHILDREN'S PUBLISHERS UK
61 – 63 Uxbridge Road, London, W5 5SA

www.**randomhouse**.co.uk
www.**randomhousechildrens**.co.uk

Addresses for companies within The Random House Group Limited
can be found at: www.randomhouse.co.uk/offices.htm
THE RANDOM HOUSE GROUP Limited Reg. No. 954009

A CIP catalogue record for this book is available
from the British Library. Printed in China

To my family, my friends,
and to all those children who won't go to sleep
without a bedtime story.

The Astonishing Case of the
STOLEN STORIES
JONATHAN CAPE
LONDON
Anca Sandu

There are many kinds of detective:
traditional detectives,

A good detective does everything by the book.

experimental
(and very handsome)
detectives,

A good detective always looks for new and original methods.

and ...

hungry detectives.

A good detective does not solve cases on an empty stomach.

Every good detective is different and when they work together they can crack uncrackable cases and solve terribly mysterious mysteries.

So one day, when a
royal message arrived
from the king calling
the detectives to
the palace, they
were ready.

They were
always ready.

"What could this urgent matter be?" Fox pondered. "Perhaps the royal jewellery has been stolen!" purred Cat. "For all one knows, the royal cupcakes have been stolen and mischievously eaten," said Bear. "Don't be ridiculous, Bear," said Fox and Cat together.

The detectives arrived at the palace as quickly as they could. The king was waiting by the gate.

He sounded rather cross and worried.

The king told the detectives how sad the little prince was – how he could not eat, or sleep, or play.

All his bedtime stories had been stolen!

"This is more alarming than stolen jewellery."
"Or cupcakes - even chocolate cupcakes. Or muffins."
"Quiet, Bear!"
"Or macaroons, or pancakes, éclairs, biscuits..."

"We will start investigating immediately." said Fox. "First, we will take a close and professional look at the crime scene."

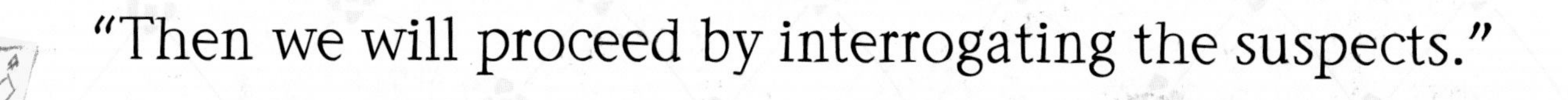

"Then we will proceed by interrogating the suspects."

The first suspect was
the big bad wolf.
"He must have eaten the
books," Bear announced.
"He is always so very hungry."

"Let us in," they called.
"Or we will huff and puff
and blow your house in!"

The detectives questioned the grumbling wolf.
"Books?" said the wolf. "I prefer pigs.
I mean, I prefer spending time with pigs."

"It seems that this time the wolf
is telling the truth,"
said Fox after conducting
a thorough search.

"The next suspect is the wicked witch," said Cat.

"As her name reveals, she is very wicked – she **must** be the thief."

"Perhaps she cooked the books in a soup," said Bear, as he investigated the witch's cauldron.

But the wicked witch had not cooked the books in a soup. How could she? Her recipe book was also missing, along with her spell book.

It seemed the thief had not stopped at bedtime stories. Books throughout the kingdom had been stolen. The detectives looked everywhere ...

But under the bridge they didn't find books. They found ...

"Books? We don't like books," said the trolls. "Books are dangerous. One of us once ate a dictionary. Now he only uses long words. He sounds rather intelligent, but it takes him for ever to finish a sentence ..."

"We don't like books.
But pirates do! Hidden islands, treasure,
talking parrots and sea monsters – they like
to read about their own adventures,"
said the trolls.
"That's it!" cried Fox. "The pirates must be the thieves!"

But the pirates had an alibi. The night the books went missing they were on an adventure of their own.

They even had treasure to prove it. Delicious treasure, which they shared with the detectives.

The detectives were no closer
to finding the missing books.

Then, as they walked,
Bear tripped ...

And found
a book.

"Once upon
a time..."
said Bear, reading
the book.

"... the detectives
found a clue!"
said Cat, finding
another book.

They found
another ...
and another ...
leading them
further and further
into the woods ...
and into the
deep, dark
cave of a big
and scary...

"Hello," said the thing.

"Who are you?" asked Fox.
"And why have you stolen
all these books?"

"Well, I don't know WHO I am,"
replied the thing. "I found everyone
else in a book, but never me –
I thought if I kept looking
I might find a book with
my story in it."

The detectives had to think
about this for a long time ...

"I've
got it!"
cried Cat.
"I know exactly
how to solve
this case."
"Have a
big party
with lots of
delicious food?"
asked Bear.

"No," said Cat. "We must write a story just for the thing."

And so Cat, Bear and Fox found a blank book, and together they wrote a very special story where the thing was the star ...

The thing's story
Once upon a time there lived a thing. But the thing didn't know what he was, and neither did anyone else. The thing was VERY BIG and unusual.
Wherever he went, people would run away in fear. The thing was so sad and lonely that he sat and cried all the time.
One day the thing heard screaming and shouting – there was a scary dragon, and it flew around setting fire to everything it saw. So the thing decided he would help.

He shouted at the dragon in
his most scary, booming voice.
"Go away!" The dragon was so
frightened that it flew away
and was never seen again.
From then on, the thing
realised that he was a hero,
and Hero became his name.
Everywhere Hero
went, he found nice things
to do for people, and
everybody loved him.
And Hero lived
happily ever after.

Hero was delighted
with his very own story,
and his new name.
But what about all
the books he
had taken?

Well, with the help of the detectives,
Hero returned every one.

"I'm sorry," Hero
said to the king.

"You are officially forgiven," said the king, "on one condition ...
Could you please help read the prince a bedtime story?"

Hero was very good at reading stories.
He had had a lot of practice! Soon the prince was fast asleep.

The detectives celebrated with some yummy cake.
"Another case successfully solved."
"Another? We've never solved one before."
ring ring
All was well in the world ...
Until the next case!